The Baby in the Window

The Baby in the Window

Jen Guyuron

gatekeeper press™
Columbus, Ohio

The Baby in the Window

Published by Gatekeeper Press
2167 Stringtown Rd, Suite 109
Columbus, OH 43123-2989
www.GatekeeperPress.com

ISBN (hardcover): 9781662906039

This book is dedicated to the most wonderful OB-GYN - Dr. Dinkar Rao - who devotes his life to every patient and baby he delivers. There are not enough words to describe how much you are appreciated.

I would also like to deeply thank my mother for her significant help making this book come to life.

Welcome home, our little one,
beautiful and new.

Our hearts are filled with love and joy
at the miracle of you.

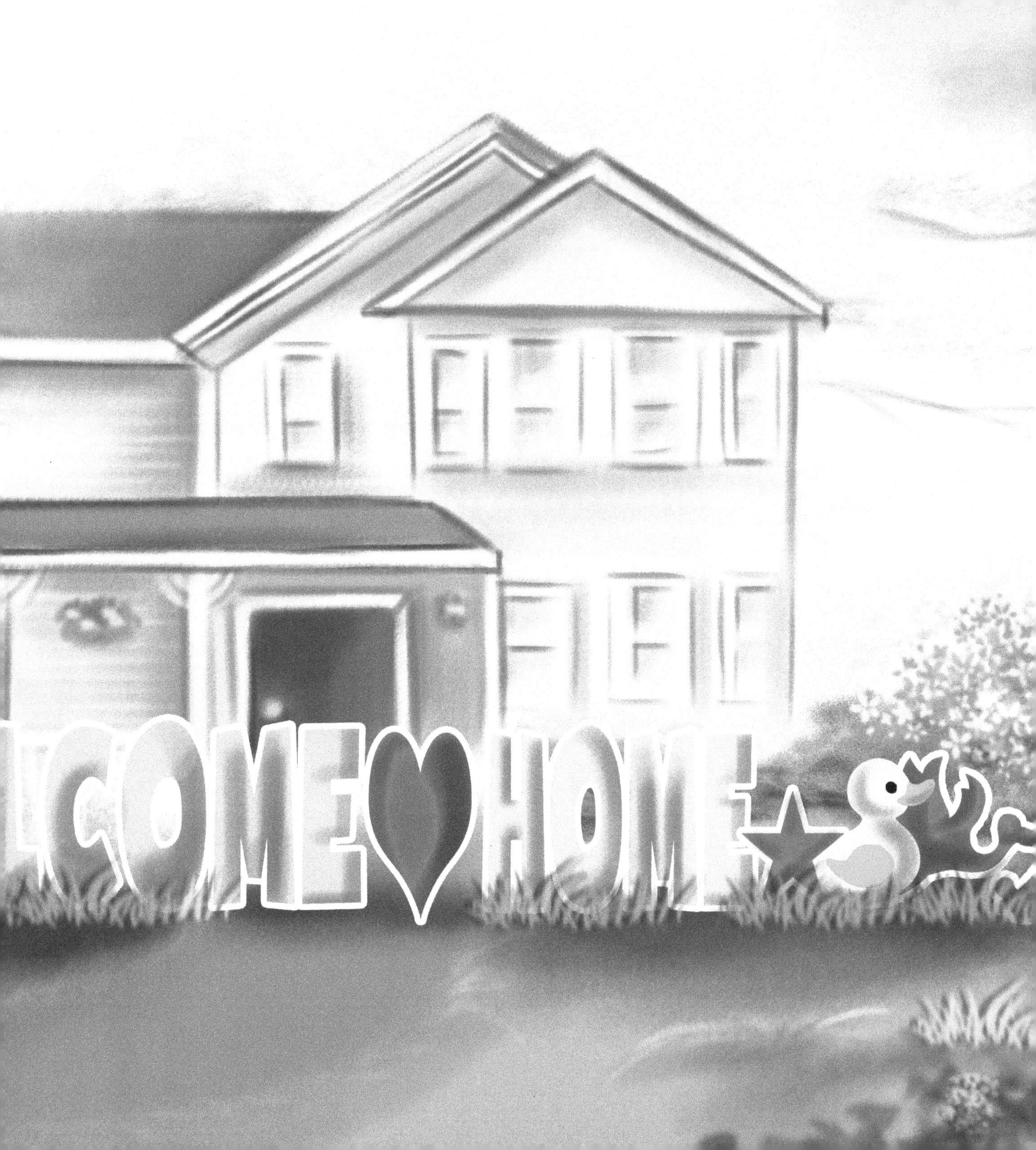
HOME

We want to give you everything,
but the world right now is strange.

The only thing we're sure of
is that every day brings change.

We're told, "Stay close to family, but stay six feet apart."

We try our best to keep this,
even though it breaks our heart.

Your cousins, aunts, and uncles
all want to come and play.

They'll meet you through the window,
but outside they'll have to stay.

It's all a new experience
as we find our way.

We have to try to make the best of each and every day.

From baking bread to planting
to tie-dying clothes,

we've had some special moments —
some highs and, yes, some lows.

The point will come, I know this,
when this will be in the past.

There will be no more quarantine,
no more distancing, and no more masks.

You will grow up quickly,
and one day you might ask
all about this crazy time
in your history class.

When this all is over,
there is so much we can do —

simple things,
like candy stores
or going to the zoo.

Going to see family,
with greetings of big hugs,

playing with our friends indoors —
these are things we love.

Baseball games and shopping trips,
lots of places to explore,

nice vacations on big ships —
all of this and even more.

We're grateful for our treasure!
The best thing we have is you,

and the sunshine that you bring us
in everything you do.

The moment our
doors can open,
we'll let our
loved ones in.

This will be a special time
when magic can begin!

We'll look back at the window
where we once sat,
but off we will go
and we won't look back.

Everyone will be together,
the way it ought to be.

The world will smile,
"It's over ...

Finally!"

Baby's First-Year Memories

Baby's name:

Born on:

Weight:

Time:

Eye color:

Hair color:

Height:

Your delivery story:

Your first visitor:

What was the world like
when you were born?

What did your siblings
(if any) think when they
met you for the first
time?

Mom's first meal
after you were born:

Baby's 1-Month Milestones:

You love ...

You dislike ...

Favorite things to do:

You are so cute when ...

Favorite song/lullaby:

Baby's 2-Month Milestones:

You love ...

You dislike ...

Favorite things
to do:

You are so
cute when ...

Favorite
song/lullaby:

Baby's 3-Month Milestones:

You love ...

You dislike ...

Favorite things to do:

You are so cute when ...

Favorite song/lullaby:

Baby's 4-Month Milestones:

You love ...

You dislike ...

Favorite things to do:

You are so cute when ...

Favorite song/lullaby:

Doctor checkup:

Height: _____ percentile

Weight: _____ percentile

Baby's 5-Month Milestones:

You love ...

You dislike ...

Favorite things to do:

You are so cute when ...

Favorite song/lullaby:

Baby's 6-Month Milestones:

You love ...

You dislike ...

Favorite things to do:

You are so cute when ...

Favorite song/lullaby:

Doctor checkup:

Height: _____ percentile

Weight: _____ percentile

Baby's 7-Month Milestones:

You love ...

You dislike ...

Favorite things to do:

You are so cute when ...

Favorite song/lullaby:

Baby's 8-Month Milestones:

You love ...

You dislike ...

Favorite things to do:

You are so cute when ...

Favorite song/lullaby:

Baby's 9-Month Milestones:

You love ...

You dislike ...

Favorite things to do:

You are so cute when ...

Favorite song/lullaby:

Doctor checkup:

Height: [   ] percentile

Weight: [   ] percentile

Baby's 10-Month Milestones:

You love ...

You dislike ...

Favorite things to do:

You are so cute when ...

Favorite song/lullaby:

Baby's 11-Month Milestones:

You love ...

You dislike ...

Favorite things to do:

You are so cute when ...

Favorite song/lullaby:

Baby's 12-Month Milestones:

You love ...

You dislike ...

Favorite things to do:

You are so cute when ...

Favorite song/lullaby:

Doctor checkup:

Height: _____ percentile

Weight: _____ percentile

It's Your Birthday!

What was the
world like today?

Who celebrated
with you?

What special food
did you eat?

What can you do
that makes people
smile?

"Your First" Dates:

Lifted head:

Rolled over:

Sat up:

Crawled:

First Step:

First Word:

CPSIA information can be obtained
at www.ICGtesting.com
Printed in the USA
BVHW020816260321
603273BV00026B/686